Robert had put his profile on the blockchain sites with mingled hope and dread. Some guys blamed their partners for losing their NookieCoin, as if their failure wasn't their fault. Everyone knew women were more complicated than men. He'd exercised religiously, going for endurance over strength. He'd read the articles and studied the videos. Robert felt certain that if he went broke and incel, it wouldn't be because he didn't prepare.

It'd be because he was terrible in bed.

The next day, after his workout, he found Mallory's message waiting.

By the Same Author:

Immortal Clay
Kipuka Blues
Butterfly Stomp Waltz
Hydrogen Sleets
git commit murder
git sync murder (coming 2018)
Bones Like Water (coming 2018)

Nonfiction (as Michael W Lucas):

Ed Mastery – SSH Mastery – Relayd and Httpd Mastery
PAM Mastery – FreeBSD Mastery: Advanced ZFS
FreeBSD Mastery: Specialty Filesystems
FreeBSD Mastery: ZFS – Tarsnap Mastery
Networking for Systems Administrators
FreeBSD Mastery: Storage Essentials – Sudo Mastery
DNSSEC Mastery – Absolute OpenBSD
Network Flow Analysis – Absolute FreeBSD
Cisco Routers for the Desperate – PGP & GPG

See your favorite bookstore for more!

Bedazzled by Blockchain

An Erotic Cryptocurrency Transaction

Michael Warren Lucas

Early readers are invaluable in improving stories. I always thank my early readers when a story gets published. In this case, though, my early readers have families to think of. I can best demonstrate my gratitude by losing their contact information and forgetting their names.

It's the least I can do. Really.

If you look at https://www.patreon.com/mwlucas, you'll see that a few folks send me money every month in exchange for getting their name in all of my books. I suspect that Kate Ebneter never expected her generosity would come back to bite her like this, but here we are.

1

Mallory had heard her whole life that putting sex on the blockchain was civilization's highest achievement.

Sitting in the plush hotel room waiting for Robert, she was beginning to doubt all of civilization.

Blockchain had been around for decades. They'd even tried using it for money, back before the Neville-Rice-Neils Theorem devastated huge swaths of cryptography. The concept of a digitally signed, unalterable ledger of transactions had been a historical curiosity until nanotech implants allowed measuring and classifying pleasure.

A post-scarcity world didn't truly *need* money, but humans *wanted* it.

The big problem with digital money was forgery, but the impulses of billions of unique human nervous systems still couldn't be forged.

She'd decorated her one bedroom apartment nicely, but the room at the One Night Holiday Inn felt almost shamefully decadent. The bed was big enough to grow a garden, the mattress thick enough to hide a body. With those pillows it looked insanely comfortable, but she hadn't touched it. The thought of what would happen on those soft blankets, soon, set her pulse fluttering for reasons having nothing to do with comfort.

The pale peach walls featured sprawling, abstract paintings that seemed designed to soothe, all gentle curves and pastel colors that simultaneously reminded her of innocence and bare limbs. A wall screen big enough to play the latest *Space Marines* at life size hung opposite the bed, silently displaying a gorgeous white-sand beach from some long-drowned tropical island. She'd pulled the sheers to block out the evening sunlight, reducing the city outside to a diffuse blur.

Mallory squeezed her bare toes into the soft carpet. She'd never felt such a well-padded floor before, and hadn't expected one here.

The room came for free, of course. Almost every hotel chain offered free rooms for people's first NookieCoin transaction, in the hope of gleaning future business from happy memories. Mallory felt pretty sure that the bottle of champagne chilling in the gleaming ice bucket would normally be an extra charge, as would the silver-domed tray.

She'd peeked under the dome. Tiny single-mouthful sandwiches, wrapped to stay fresh. Sliced strawberries. Ice cream in self-freezing cartons, with a little jar of real chocolate topping.

It all looked delicious.

She had no appetite.

Instead, she kept thinking about the creepy old raisin who'd taught Introductory Modern Economics in junior high. She could still remember his sing-song droning voice. *Cryptocurrencies grow by proving you've performed labor. In the old days people generated proof-of-work through mathematical computations. Today, the biomedical networks we're all fitted with at birth allow us to measure pleasure, generating proof-of-ecstasy even as they provide the social benefit of separating long-term relationships from sexual intercourse.*

She'd giggled with the rest of the class.

And every time she'd had a clumsy experiment with one of her male friends, she'd imagined the nanomolecular computational mesh laced through her lighting up in parallel with her nerves.

Really, those friends hadn't lit up her nerves very much.

She'd kept hearing that men were simpler, but she wasn't too certain she'd done well either.

Modern society used blockchain-verified proof-of-ecstasy as currency. Everyone got enough dole to survive, but if you wanted more? During a transaction you swapped a chunk of your NookieCoin and split the profit from proof-of-ecstasy.

Or losses, if someone didn't enjoy the transaction.

Theoretically, a successful transaction would generate enough proof-of-ecstasy to cover the hotel room, the meal, and more.

Maybe much more, if they shot the moon.

On her first transaction, though, she'd be lucky to break even.

Mallory's sister Alice had told her to relax. To enjoy what happened. To forget about the implants, and profitability, and just enjoy whatever the evening offered. Supposedly a night arranged through an exchange was completely different than school-age fumbling with friends.

Should she have set up music? Maybe something almost subliminal? No, that would be cheesy. She had no idea what modern music Robert liked, and she'd never physically met anyone who liked the Ugandan Federation dubsqueak she binged on. She could go for twen-cen, to match her outfit, but that stuff was such a mixed mess of good and bad, and every last bit of it was in dreary four-four time. The tropical scene on the wall screen was already tacky, but the room had been too silent and still when she'd arrived. The beach feed was a lot more subtle than the hotel's infinite supply of streaming porn.

Mallory reminded herself had no reason to worry. She'd found Robert on a reputable exchange. They were both twenty years old. Both had the complete NookieCoins they'd been issued at birth, not yet sliced up by transactions. While some people started selling off their coins as soon as they hit eighteen, trading the irreplaceable for trendy toys or, worse, blowing everything in a series of badly considered transactions, Robert was as financially conservative as Mallory.

That bode well.

When they'd met for coffee yesterday, he'd been more attractive than his profile video. Muscular without being muscle-bound. Clean hands with neatly trimmed nails. Clear green eyes, strong cheekbones. Fresh breath. He'd been formal and polite, trying really hard not to stare at her cleavage even as they'd talked through their agreement. He was a little bigger than her, tall enough that he could just about rest his chin on her forehead and broader through the chest.

He'd been exactly as nervous as her.

Maybe she should have chosen someone with a blockchain-backed journal of successful transactions.

But something in Robert's profile had kept drawing her back. The deepness of his voice? The strong chin? The way he kept his gaze casually steady when so many people either avoided meeting the camera or kept a creepy fixed stare?

Some people negotiated a complete script beforehand, but Mallory thought that felt even more unnatural. They'd agreed to get together and see what happened, letting each back out any time. Sitting here, she couldn't help wondering how far they were going to go. His lips on hers, sure. Caressing and touching? Of course. His hand on her clit? Maybe his mouth? Hands wouldn't feed their implants much neural activity, generating less proof-of-ecstasy and thus less profit, but the risks were a lot lower.

Or would she find herself pulling him into her? Down her throat? She didn't mind doing that, but didn't exactly enjoy it either. All the way into her? That could be the best… or the worst, depending on the man.

She could still back out. Just this morning, she'd received a last-minute offer to exchange her intact coin for a luxurious private seaside villa in temperate Greenland. That plus the dole would keep her comfortable for her life. The buyer would even pay Robert the cancellation fee, to keep her coin whole.

But with zero NookieCoin, the only partners she'd attract would be others who'd opted out of civilization.

Or those who'd so thoroughly failed to satisfy a series of partners that they'd burned through their dwindling NookieCoin and gone incel.

And twenty, plus or minus a year or two, was the traditional age for joining the blockchain. Everyone needed a few fumbling years with whoever they found before, sure. Waiting too long made you seem a radical, troubled, or perhaps even a crypto-anarchist who wanted to go back to the nightmare days of artificial scarcity, government money, and random sex.

In the coffee shop, her nano-implants had interrogated Robert's and verified their compatibility.

His cheeks had flushed when he suggested a point-one NookieCoin swap. Enough to show he was serious, but modest enough that even total loss wouldn't ruin either of them. Most people were willing to give you a try so long as you had more than half a coin and your recent history had shown improvement.

All solid and sensible and tidy.

If tonight went well, they might generate ten percent on the transaction, point oh-one NkC in a couple hours.

If it went very well, she might shoot the moon and become wealthy.

Still, nervousness made her fidget. The chair didn't have arms to grip, so she squeezed her thighs through the cotton dress. She'd worn the prettiest dress she owned, great big red roses laid one over the other, and complemented it with a spritz of flowery perfume.

But maybe Robert wouldn't like it? It was awfully twen-cen.

Mallory took a deep breath and deliberately relaxed her shoulders, stroking her dress to smooth the fabric. He'd seemed honestly interested in what she said, and wasn't that the important part? She caressed the strand of natural pearls around her neck, a relic from her great-grandmother she'd worn as a token of luck.

The pearls. The dress. It was all too much.

She should have worn something from this century.

Or skipped clothes entirely. Welcomed him at the door wearing her pearls and a smile. Maybe a couple of strategically placed rhinestones. She could still—

Someone rapped lightly on the door.

Her throat froze.

The hotel announced in its smooth voice, "Robert Pumali."

Mallory almost leapt to her feet, instinctively glancing at the mirror over the minibar. Hair? Cut to a neat inch and tapered at the back, without much room to go wrong but still tidy. Skin? Clean, tanned, with a lingering touch of gleam from moisturizer. Dress—a wrinkle? A quick swipe down her side eased it away. She couldn't help grinning widely to see if her straight white teeth had somehow gone crooked, or if yesterday's broccoli had made a magical reappearance despite having brushed twice in the last hour.

How was this supposed to work?

Was Robert going to tromp in and leap at her?

It might be easiest if he did.

Don't mess this up, Mallory. She blinked one eye, then the other, twice, engaging her nano-implants' command mode. "Blockchain computation start." She felt unchanged, but knew that the fine mesh of microscopic machinery inside her had started processing every nerve signal. The machinery that would keep her healthy for centuries might grant her wealth.

Heart pounding, the coppery taste of adrenalin in the back of her throat, Mallory opened the door.

To her shock, Robert looked just as retro as she did.

He'd dressed in a lightweight suit in dark blue pinstripe. He had gleaming black shoes with laces. They couldn't be real leather, but they looked good. The pants didn't quite hug his legs, but she found the hints of muscle beneath them far more enticing than the more modern blatant fashion. The open sport coat exposed a slice of white button-down shirt tucked into the waist, a narrow vision somehow promising tight abs.

He'd worn a thin, bright red necktie. Most people didn't know how to tie one. She had no idea.

Robert's face had smooth skin over taut pale skin and fierce cheekbones. His full, pale lips twitched upon seeing her, green eyes turning even brighter. His hair was a little too long and tousled to really match the outfit, but it looked really good on him. Both hands cradled a wine bottle.

An actual, glass wine bottle.

Mallory stopped.

Any wine that came in glass bottles cost at least two weeks of dole. Not dole-after-paying-for-room-and-food, but two weeks raw dole.

Maybe he was conservative with his NookieCoin birthright, but saving one's dole took a whole extra level of commitment.

Had Robert blown his savings for tonight?

Mallory's nervousness dissolved into a tingle in her fingertips, her cheeks, even her toes. Curiosity flashed through her—did the implants catch that feeling and feed it to their computations? Could boring math

14

capture and checksum this ethereal rush?

She reached out to tug at the faintly coarse fabric of Robert's sleeve, drawing him through the door before he said a word. His lips were parted as if he was about to say something, but when she placed her hands over his lapels he sucked the words right back through his parted lips. Mallory felt hard muscle even through the layered cloth.

Forget agreements and transactions and the whole basis-of-civilization thing. Robert thought she was worth sacrifices. In an age when everybody had everything they truly needed, only needing money for luxuries, the thought sparked warmth deep inside her.

It wasn't heat.

Not yet.

But it could be soon.

Mallory slid her hands up Robert's firm chest, around the back of his neck, up into his curly hair, and pulled him down into a kiss.

His mouth seemed paralyzed for half a second, just long enough for his body to overthrow surprise, then his smooth lips moved with hers. She'd caught him with his mouth a fraction open, and took full advantage to let the tip of her tongue brush against that little space.

Robert's soft, deep groan made her insides flutter. That secret warmth flared and spread, making her hands reflexively knot in his hair.

His kiss demanded nothing. He seemed to be enjoying the kiss for exactly what it was, right in the moment, eagerly accepting what she offered and returning it. His tongue brushed hers, slowly sliding past to barely caress her lips.

Between them, his hands shifted the wine bottle.

Mallory pulled him closer, pinning his hands and the bottle between them. Not hard enough to hurt, but firm enough to say she wanted him exactly there.

After an endless moment Mallory eased back, letting the kiss fade into a brush of lips on lips, then a millimeter gap. His breath tasted clean and minty, with just a hint of cinnamon. "Hi."

"Hi." Robert's whisper teased her lips.

If nervous signals fed the blockchain, their implants had to be computing a torrent from the kiss alone.

Mallory released Robert's hair, and eased back to pluck the wine bottle from his hands. "Let me put this on ice."

2

Robert stared at Mallory's back, transfixed, as she walked across the plush carpet to the ice bucket.

The pearls around Mallory's neck cut a white line across her smooth tan skin. Skin that ran down to just below the shoulder blades, where the dress took over. He felt dimly aware of the pretty fabric of the dress, how the outfit somehow went with his retro suit, but that knowledge felt distant. Those bare shoulders and upper back hit him like hot iron, sending heat down his spine straight into his cock.

They'd had an agreement, yes, but she could withdraw any time.

And he ached with a desperate need to touch Mallory's strong, soft shoulders.

Then all the rest of her.

Robert had put his profile on the blockchain sites with mingled hope and dread. Some guys blamed their partners for losing their NookieCoin, as if their failure wasn't their fault. Everyone knew women were more complicated than men. He'd exercised religiously, going for endurance over strength. He'd read the articles and studied the videos. Robert felt certain that if he went broke and incel, it wouldn't be because he didn't prepare.

It'd be because he was terrible in bed.

The next day, after his workout, he found Mallory's message waiting.

Heart pounding, throat blocked with curiosity and possibilities, he'd delayed listening to it until he got home rather than having his implants dump it into his brain. He wanted the real first impression, through his senses, not a machine-driven abstraction.

At some level he'd anticipated the exchange would match him up with a plain looking woman. He'd seen his face in the mirror every morning, and even when he studied himself with charitable eyes he didn't see anything remarkable. He cleaned up okay. He flossed regularly, polished the callus off his feet, trimmed away inconvenient or unappealing hair. He wasn't ugly, but he sure wasn't handsome.

Trembling, he'd opened Mallory's message in the privacy of his apartment.

Mallory's mere image locked his brain up. That soft jaw. Full, strong but soft-looking lips. Her rich brown eyes burned out of the screen, and her faint hint of a smile seemed to promise something beyond mere sex.

17

Her voice had hit sparks. *Hi! I'm Mallory. Want to get lunch? Coffee?* She'd sounded impossibly cheerful and confident.

Excited and terrified, he'd almost forgotten to check the exchange ratings before messaging back.

According to the comparative biometric data gathered by their implants, they had a nearly miraculous ninety percent compatibility. Only an approximation, true, but the best estimate any system could generate before a fully logged transaction.

Robert tried eight times to record a response that didn't sound like a total idiot.

In the days between arranging that first meeting and the actual date, the mere memory of Mallory's face had been a welcome intruder. Sometimes he'd go as long as a minute without wondering what that first meeting would be like. Would he put his foot in his mouth five seconds in? Or would it take a whole five minutes?

When Mallory had walked into the coffee bar, he'd realized that the recording hadn't done her justice. She'd worn a touch of honeysuckle perfume, just enough to penetrate the sharp smells of coffee. Her voice sounded like velvet over steel, gentle but ready to turn fierce at need. Lush rosebud lips that demanded kissing. Hair cropped unstylishly short. When she'd turned her head he'd seen how she'd cut her hair to expose the back of her neck, and he couldn't help imagining kissing her right below the hairline. Down her spine.

He'd practiced his NookieCoin proposal, but delivering it with his cock straining painfully at his jeans had demanded all his concentration. Yes, everybody hooked up after school sometimes, but picking someone based on their looks and personality was more awkward than anything. What did looks or charm have to do with sex?

Through the whole discussion Mallory had watched him more carefully than anyone ever had, probably wondering all the things women had always wondered about men.

When they'd reached agreement and she'd stood to leave, he'd stood as well. The flash in her eyes told him she knew about those old-style manners, and appreciated them.

He'd felt the urge to kiss her then—but no. Everything he'd read said, save everything for the transaction.

He'd watched her walk away. He couldn't remember what she'd worn to the coffee shop, but he remembered how her hips shifted at each step.

He hadn't stopped thinking about her. Getting to sleep last night had demanded a long, icy-cold shower.

And today?

At least his outfit had gone over well. She knew about old-style manners, so he'd taken a risk with his retro suit. He'd blown his entire savings on the best bottle of wine he could get.

A foolish expense for one night? Probably.

But his swollen lips burned and tingled with the echoes of her kiss.

The muscles of Mallory's back flexed as she tugged the champagne from the bucket of ice. Ice crunched as she tried to slip Robert's wine back into the resulting crater, but that never worked. The dress hugged her

19

form, highlighting an ass that begged to be squeezed, the knee-length skirt inviting him to slide his hands up her thighs.

Robert had always talked things through with girls. What did they want? How did they want it? What did they like?

Often, they barely knew.

But here, with Mallory, in this insanely decadent hotel room, was totally different. They both knew what they were here for.

The exchange said they were compatible.

Compatibility meant that the things he wanted to do were the things she would like.

And he *needed* to start on those shoulders.

Patience, he reminded himself. The biggest mistake men made in a transaction was rushing. Wham-bam-thankyoumaʼam went out with scarcity.

Robert walked up behind Mallory as she dug in the ice and turned the wine bottle. When he touched her shoulder, Mallory let out a little breath. Not quite a gasp. His own shoulders trembled at the feeling of her soft, hot skin under his fingertips, but he forced himself to slowly trace the line of her shoulders up to the line of pearls.

He lowered his mouth to the other shoulder and planted one kiss.

The taste of her clean sweet skin inflamed his fire. Excitement blurred his vision and fogged his thoughts. With careful deliberation, he placed one hand over her hip and put a second kiss a little further up Malloryʼs shoulder, letting his other hand trace back down the other shoulder.

Mallory hissed, seized the hand on her hip and clamped it firmly over her tit.

Even through the dress, the motion electrified Robert. Her tit was a little too big for his hand, overflowing in all the right ways. Her heat seemed to burn through the dress to his palm. She felt firm and, somehow, simultaneously soft.

Wait.

Beneath that dress… was she wearing an actual *bra*?

Most women wore invisibly thin nano-based supports, even in cosplay, but Mallory had taken the old-fashioned dress all the way to her skin.

Robert's breath quickened even further. His heart rapped impatiently at the inside of his ribs. His hand would have trembled, but the weight of her hand squeezing his against didn't leave his fingers space to move.

Patience didn't mean standing there like he'd been hit in the head. Even if he felt like he'd been hit in the head.

Robert slipped his other hand around Mallory's stomach, easing her back to him. His mouth moved a fraction of an inch, letting him kiss unexplored skin while his trapped hand gently squeezed.

Mallory's groan was deep and strong enough to reach him through her spine, his chest, vibrating straight to his heart even as the sound hit his ears.

He needed her. He had to have Mallory. Right now, naked and begging and wrapped around him. His patience felt like a frayed rope, barely anchoring him to reason. He squeezed her tighter to conceal his trembling, opened his mouth, and gently nipped where Mallory's succulent shoulders met her graceful exposed neck.

Mallory's hand over his squeezed harder on her tit, demanding more. Thrilled, he obliged, kissing and gnawing and tasting every morsel of exposed shoulder, the back of her neck, his hand massaging her. He ached to squeeze more forcefully, but she'd demonstrated how much pressure she wanted. Her fingers still cradled his, encouraging his touch, guiding him to caress her exactly as she wanted.

No harder than that. He was giving, not taking.

Maybe a little harder? No, that might hurt. The line between pleasure and pain was too narrow. If she'd wanted pain, the exchange wouldn't have matched them.

Mallory shuddered. The finger she traced over his arm trembled.

Robert shifted his head to the other side of her neck, laying a fresh line of kisses and eliciting a fresh gasp from Mallory. The hand pinning him to her tit relaxed.

Impulsively, Robert spun Mallory around and pulled her to him. Her mouth was hotter than before, her lips firmer and hungrier against his. He wanted everything. Now. He kept his motions slow, though, easing his tongue out to glide across her lips.

Mallory's mouth opened, her tongue thrusting out exactly the way Robert wanted it to, caressing and tangling with his to send fresh sparks through his soul. Mallory felt better pressed up against him fully dressed than some girls had fully naked.

Her arms wrapped around Robert, pulling them even closer together, wrapping them together incredibly tightly. His whole body buzzed when the bulge of his cock brushed her stomach.

He felt Mallory smile through the kiss.

Then she leaned into his cock. Hard.

Robert's groan traveled from the bottom of his being straight into Mallory's mouth.

Mallory's arms slid out from around him, her hands leaving desolate trails even as his own grip tightened. He felt her arms twist around behind her, her hands pushing his out of her way.

The zipper. She wanted the zipper on her dress.

Robert slid his hands down to the small of her back and kept going, until he just touched the slope of the top of Mallory's ass.

Her tongue surged forward to caress the roof of his mouth.

Robert's hands swept down and seized her ass as he heard the low buzz of a Mallory drawing her zipper. Her tongue gave one last flick of his lips, then she tugged back, letting the kiss fade from a bruise to a brush to feather-light. His lips felt so swollen that he felt certain they should reach the fraction of an inch that separated them.

Her hands rose to his sides, caressing his ribs. "That's… promising."

Robert's heart beat so hard, if he talked it might leap up his throat and escape. His blood whooshed in his ears, and the smell of honeysuckle filled him. Somehow, he managed a nod.

The exchange system had been right. They were crazy compatible.

He had to slow down. His cock felt ready to rupture his pants and then rupture itself.

Mallory gave a tiny, wicked smile as her hands traced up and down his ribcage. "Let go of me."

Robert needed a breath to make sense of the words. Had he done something wrong? That tight ass filling his hands—had he pushed too far? No, Mallory's smile said she wasn't angry.

He needed all his willpower to pull his hands forward, trading her ass for her hips, sliding his palms free, releasing her one knuckle at a time until only the tips of his fingers brushed her hips.

Releasing her felt like breaking something inside him.

Mallory's smile grew. She stepped to the side, putting a couple more feet between them. Raised her arms.

Without that support, the unzipped dress plunged to the floor.

Robert could only stare.

She'd taken the outfit all the way to her skin. That white bra with the lace trim was right out of a twen-cen costumer's catalog. And he felt pretty sure those were actual Hanes-style briefs.

In between them, though, Mallory's exposed skin shone glorious. Even the strand of pearls circling her neck fascinated him.

She stepped out of fallen dress. "You stay right there."

"Sure." Robert would happily stare at her all day. Hungrily, but happily. His hands twitched with the desperate hunger to touch her every curve.

Mallory's smile flickered. "You like what you see?"

Was that a hint of uncertainty in her voice? "I like it a whole lot," he whispered. "Maybe you should show me the rest. Just to be sure."

Her smile steadied. "I need to pick up this dress first. You stay exactly there."

Mouth dry as paper, Robert didn't trust himself to speak. He nodded. He suddenly realized just how warm he felt inside the suit. Modern fabric or not, he was steaming inside this outfit. One hand reached up to his tie.

"Don't do that," Mallory whispered. "Leave the tie on. Leave everything just like that."

For the sound of Mallory's voice, talking to him like that, Robert would happily steam to death. "Anything you want."

"Anything?" Mallory took half a step closer to him, then turned around.

Wrapped in those old-fashioned undies, that ass looked just as amazing as it had felt.

Fire had spread to Robert's every fiber. His implants had to be busier than they'd ever been, metering and hashing every signal that zapped through his overloaded nerves.

But then Mallory somehow reached behind her to get at back of her bra. Robert wasn't sure his own arms could have duplicated that maneuver.

Let alone when she used those long, delicate fingers to edge the bra hooks apart.

The cloth fell away, exposing the perfect lines of her back. The broad swell of her shoulders falling to a waist strong and thick enough to be worth holding, spreading to wide hips that promised to swallow a man, all trailing down into strong, lithe legs and perfect heels sunk into the carpet.

Robert felt ready to fall to his knees before her. To plunge onto her. To adore every inch of her, inside and out, over and over again with his eyes, his fingers, his lips, his tongue.

He dragged his eyes back up. Mallory was looking over her shoulder to watch his face. He probably looked like an idiot, standing there with blatant ravenous lust sprayed across his features, but at least it wiped away any uncertainty he might have seen in her face.

Then she backed up half a step, putting herself exactly at arm's length.

Bent over to pick up the dress.

Her ass, concealed enticingly by the thin layer of cotton, shifted and wiggled. She had to be doing that on purpose.

Robert couldn't help reaching out to brush a fingertip against the cotton.

Mallory said, "Don't move those feet."

Without interrupting her chore, Mallory shifted back a critical couple of inches. She was just barely too far away for him to place his whole hand on her ass, but by turning he could let the fingers of his right hand freely caress her through the cotton, tracing up the concealed crack and down the other side.

Mallory made a sound somewhere between a hum and a purr, swinging her hips just enough to encourage his exploration.

Was that already a tiny wet patch in her undies? Robert's heart jackhammered. He had never felt so thoroughly aroused. Keeping himself in place as she'd asked exhausted his willpower. He couldn't prevent himself from trailing his fingers down towards the patch of cotton that only barely concealed the pussy he so completely wanted.

She gasped at the touch.

And yes, she was already wet.

For a precious, treasured second, her body rocked forward, lifting her ass, bringing her cloaked clit right against his fingertips.

Robert's breath stopped. His necktie might have been a noose.

An endless second passed.

Then Mallory shifted forward, away from his trailing fingers.

The room seemed to spin.

Air. He'd forgotten to breathe.

He forced his lungs to move.

When Mallory turned around, her face was flushed and her breathing hard and fast—not quick, not yet. Just fast.

Robert desperately needed to make her breathe quickly. He needed to make her gasp. Cry out.

Scream. Beg. Simultaneously.

"Do you want the underwear too?" Mallory's voice trembled.

Her nipples rose from broad areolae in tits that left him aching. He didn't even try to look away. "Yes."

Mallory's thumbs slipped into the waistband, right beneath that perfect bellybutton, and eased the elastic down a critical inch.

Robert's gaze fixated on her exposed pubis.

Pale. Tender.

Begging to be kissed.

Promising even more tenderness below.

Mallory's voice didn't merely tremble. It shook. She barely whispered, "I've always wanted to be worshipped by a really well dressed man."

Robert wrenched his eyes back up to those succulent, kissable lips. Lips that were only the beginning. "Get on the bed, and I will adore every last inch."

3

Mallory found getting into the bed proved more difficult than it should have been. Robert's gaze alone had almost devoured her. His touch had transformed her insides to quivering jelly, and his kiss had flooded her with lust. The layers and layers of thin blankets on the bed seemed designed to annoy, and the mattress felt too soft to scoot across.

She felt pretty sure that the mattress wasn't really for sleeping on. She knew the sheets were soft, all sheets were soft, but after Robert's gentle touch they felt close to rough against her back. She could feel how tightly he controlled himself. The way he held her, the way his tongue rasped ravenously against hers, the way he pulled her close and wrapped himself around her, everything about him screamed that he thirsted for her like he'd been in the desert for days. His struggle to control himself couldn't be more obvious. He wanted her—not just the way any horny twenty-year-old wanted a woman. When she'd undone her bra, his eyes had almost exploded from his skull.

Something about her, personally, inflamed Robert's lust just short of madness.

And yet, he thought Mallory was worth restraining himself for.

It wasn't just the NookieCoin transaction, either. Mallory felt pretty sure Robert hadn't thought about finances since she'd grabbed his hand and clasped it over her breast. He was totally different than the polite but anxious boy she'd met yesterday.

He was exactly as polite today. But a different kind of polite.

And a whole different kind of man.

And now he was standing by the bed. Almost looming. The size difference that had seemed so minor yesterday had taken extra dimensions. He'd straightened the lapels of the suit jacket and disciplined the tie. She'd thoughtlessly popped out that line about wanting a well-dressed man, and he delivered.

That complicated, old-fashioned suit, though?

He'd thought Mallory was worth dressing up for.

And when she'd guided his hands, he'd obeyed.

Right now, she could see how watching her arrange a pillow behind her head consumed his entire attention. His gaze moved up and down her body, staring at her hands and her stomach and even her legs with the same hunger he showed when studying her breasts.

He said he wanted everything.

Watching his incredibly focused attention work up her shins to her knees, Mallory realized that he really meant *everything*.

She hardly knew Robert.

Before he'd shown up today, she'd thought they might stop at petting.

Her willingness to offer him everything he could take with his clothes on surprised her.

Her body had its own ideas, though. She'd felt excitement before, sure, but her breasts ached for Robert's touch. Her nipples had grown just short of painful hard, and she didn't care if they full-on hurt so long as he *touched* them. Kissed them. Suckled. Anything. She'd been excited before, sure, but when she'd tugged off the silly retro underwear she'd been shocked at just how wet they were. Watching Robert watch her kept her own lust zinging through her, a nearly electrical charge that tingled over every inch of exposed skin.

And Robert's gaze exposed her more than ever before.

She'd barely settled herself when Robert flung himself at her.

His massive male body seemed to go from upright to dominating her without traversing any of the space between them. His elbow landed next to her head, that hand slipping behind her head so his fingers could twine through her short hair, while the other sank into the mattress next to her opposite ribcage. The suddenness triggered just a flash of—not fear, not exactly, more of a hyper-awareness of Robert's extra muscle mass and that six inches of height, but then his mouth plunged to hers and she forgot everything but the way he tasted and the way his lips moved against her and how his tongue running along her gums sparked shivers all through her.

One hand cradling the back of her head, his weight on that elbow, his other hand trailed gently across her stomach. The strong fingers of his other hands trailed lazy spirals around her bellybutton, rising to trace her ribcage. Mallory wanted to slide down, to bring her breasts up to Robert's maddeningly patient touch, but his passionate, constant kisses pinned her in place.

His fingers brushed the bottom of her breast.

She couldn't help whimpering.

Robert drew the kiss to an end, pulling back to watch her face. She'd never seen a more serious expression.

She started to raise her head to draw him back into the kiss, but then his thumb brushed her nipple. Instant electricity made her mouth and eyes drop open together, the universe contracting until it contained nothing except Robert's touch and his face and meaningless haze beyond.

"That's what I want to see," Robert murmured.

He kissed her once more, quick, his mouth massaging her trembling lips. Before she could nudge his lips open, though, he pulled back and planted a kiss right at the edge of her ribs.

She dissolved under a barrage of kisses and touches that worked their way across her, up her side, around her breasts. Robert's mouth closing over one nipple ripped a gasp from her. His tongue circled only long enough to stop her breath, then he moved to her neck, her side, across her stomach, only for his tongue to alight hummingbird-light on the other nipple and electrify her again. She cradled his head with one hand, holding him there while the other stroked across his suit-covered jacket.

Telling him to keep his clothes on had sounded fun, and safe, but her whole body burned to throw away safety and let Robert consume her. She tried to tell him to get rid of them, but his probing tongue ripped her words away.

Then his free hand brushed along the side of her pussy, caressing the bare skin right outside the crack. Her gasp was more of a cry, a wordless mewling of need.

Robert raised his head. "I like that." Lust thickened his voice, and his maddening patient fingertips traced up the other side of her crack. That tiny pressure seemed to pound down her nerves, making her clit ache and her inner walls quiver and tighten.

"Clothes," she choked.

Robert crooked one side of his mouth up in a smile. "Yes?"

That light finger started tracing straight down over her crack.

Mallory surged her hips up a precious inch, opening herself around Robert's finger, pulling him into her wetness right above her clit and sending spikes of pleasure straight up her spine. Robert's eyes snapped wide, and he immediately slid that finger a precious half-inch.

Right where she wanted it.

Smooth circles of delight rolled out of Mallory's center with each circle of Robert's hand. He knew exactly how to move around her, constant counterclockwise strokes with featherweight pressure, but she needed—

"More," she gasped.

"All you want," Robert said, the serious line of his mouth belied by the delight in his eyes.

"Little harder. Just a little."

"Like that?"

"Ooooh."

"I'll take that as a yes."

"Don't stop."

"I won't."

Mallory needed a breath to find her arm. Another to find the hand on the end of it. Her fingers fluttered and trembled like Robert's hand was a downed power line, but she managed to draw it up to the dangling red line of his tie. "Lose it."

"Lose the tie?"

"Tie. Shirt. Everything."

"I'm kind of busy here." The delicious slow circles around her clit quickened a fraction. "Can't get undressed with one hand."

Thinking felt like scooping sand off a creek bed, where the current flushed everything away before she could bring her thoughts to the surface. Each circling motion flooded her thoughts away. She'd seen old movies where men pulled off their neckties. Nothing to it.

That double strand of shiny red silk dangled from Robert's neck.

One quick tug and she could throw the offending thing across the room. The jacket wasn't buttoned, she could rip it off his shoulders. If the buttons on the shirt gave her any trouble, they'd pop off. Then his pants.

He could keep the socks.

For now.

She flung her arms up, snatched the tie, and pulled.

The tie didn't come off.

Robert's circling hand seized and pushed into her, a little too hard, then flew away.

His mouth dropped open, his face instantly a little red.

Embarrassment shattered Mallory's passion, shattering the moment.

She'd pulled the tie wrong.

Robert grabbed at the tie, digging his fingers beneath the cloth.

Mallory pulled her hands back. Her pulse thudded in her ears, and she felt a sudden flush that had nothing to do with lust.

Strangled him—and she'd blown the whole transaction.

Could she help? Should she help?

No, she'd ruined everything already.

Their implants were recording it all.

Her total humiliation was going on the blockchain, for the whole world to know. Nobody would see exactly what had happened, it's not like the journal had video so they'd only know that she'd wrecked her first night and every exchange she joined would flag her with a great big warning.

Robert pulled the tie out, drawing in a deep breath.

At least she hadn't hurt him.

Mallory pulled her legs together, wrapping herself in her arms right below her breasts. "I'm sorry."

Robert heaved out. "It's okay." He smiled and inhaled again.

Maybe she could just die here. "Are you all right?"

"Really." Robert shook his shoulders, then rose to kneel. "And I'm sorry."

"What for?"

Robert shrugged out of his jacket. "For not listening."

The flush of embarrassment wasn't just on her face. Her whole body felt too warm. She must be bright red. "You've done nothing but listen."

Robert's hands shook as he attacked the buttons on his shirt. Was he that worried. "You wanted my clothes off. And I teased you."

She couldn't die from embarrassment, but maybe she could fade into invisibility? "I shouldn't have tried to rip it off you."

Robert paused, his shirt unbuttoned just enough to display a narrow V of muscular chest. "You wanted me naked so badly that you almost killed me ripping my clothes off? Miss Mallory…" He smiled. "Do you have any idea how fucking hot that is?"

He tugged his shirt the rest of the way off and flung it after the jacket.

Mallory's breath caught.

Modern implants could keep excess fat away, and ensure reasonable muscle tone. Robert had gone way past reasonable muscle tone, though, straight into holostar territory. Not the kind of testosterone-choked abs that could play Ping-Pong between themselves, but smooth solid lines that gave his chest and abs texture and definition.

He spent time and effort on his body, and it showed.

Oh, did it show.

Mallory swallowed.

Robert swept his gaze down her body again, one hand on his meticulously polished chrome belt buckle. "There's an old treatment for trouble breathing." His voice had gotten heavy again.

"Oh?"

Robert dropped his hands from his belt buckle and threw himself forward.

Mallory felt that rush at the impending impact, but he caught himself inches from her.

He brought his face close enough to hers so that his eyes filled her vision. The breath of his whisper stroked her lips. "Yeah. You need to perform mouth-to-mouth on me."

Mallory made herself relax her shoulders. She'd screwed up a moment, but maybe she hadn't blown the whole transaction.

If anything, she'd made him feel even more wanted.

His naked chest, inches from her breasts, radiated more heat than she'd ever felt from another person.

She slowly wrapped one arm around his back, using her fingers to trace lines of muscle. She slid the other behind his head, fingers tangling in his hair.

Somehow, his hair was no more mussed than when he'd come to the door.

She'd have to fix that.

With a single, convulsive squeeze, Mallory pulled Robert to her.

The last thing she remembered thinking was how smooth and hot and hard his bare skin felt pressed up against hers. Then her mind dissolved in the sensation of Robert's mouth on hers, his arms sliding beneath her to clench her back and pull her into him as if desire could pull their hearts through their ribcages and into one space. He tasted impossibly alive, that tiny hint of cinnamon he'd used detracting from his own clean breath. Every kiss across her mouth, her cheek, her neck made her gasp.

She wrapped her free leg around his.

The bastard had left his pants on.

Mallory caressed his calf with hers. When Robert bent to delightfully gnaw at her neck, she moaned, "Pants. Lose them."

Robert made a little laugh. "You want me to take my pants off?"

"Gods, yes."

"I've listened to you." She could hear the smile in his voice. "You told me to stand, I stood. I had your incredible ass in my hands, right where I wanted you, and you took it away. Right where I wanted you." His voice grew fiercer. "I need something from you."

The overwhelming desire in his voice made Mallory shiver.

Robert shifted his weight so he could lift Mallory with one arm, freeing the other. "And you are going to lie right there and let me enjoy you."

Mallory nodded. Whatever he wanted he could have.

So long as he lost the damned pants.

Lightning-fast, Robert slid down her body.

She let his hands nudge her legs apart.

He rolled between them, spreading gentle kisses along the inside of her thigh as he went, trailing sparks of pleasure. His hands slid beneath her ass, slipping a couple fingers into that crack even as his mouth descended on her clit.

Mallory's gasp was almost a hoot, a long-drawn inhalation that rode her arching back. The flick of his tongue sent shocks through her that made her hands clench the mattress.

Robert's tongue explored her, triggering shudders of pleasure that rippled out from her center. Her breath caught, making her head whirl until she could choke in another gulp of air. The world shrank again, becoming smaller than the room, smaller than the bed, smaller than even her. The only thing she felt was Robert's tongue, circling steadily, stirring an inexorable cyclone of pleasure that surged higher and higher.

"Don't stop," she choked.

Was that a laugh? Maybe it was. But that tongue never stopped.

Mallory wrapped her ankles behind Robert's head, opening herself as widely as she could. Offering herself to the pleasure he demanded of her as the pressure within her built, and built again, a tension that swelled an unstoppably as storm clouds.

And in moments, the cyclone overwhelmed her.

Spiraling waves of ecstasy rocketed through her, flashing like lightning out from her clit and up her spine, spasming down her legs and setting her interlocked ankles drumming against Robert's spine. His tongue never stopped, pinning her in place, ripples rising within her and bursting one after the other, until her body couldn't contain them any more and she wordlessly cried out, emptying her body of air and he still wouldn't stop, that merciless tongue still drawing circles.

Only when she collapsed back on the bed, quivering helplessly, did Robert's tongue release her.

The fierceness of her orgasm left Mallory scoured clean. When she inhaled, her lungs barely had the strength to raise her ribs. She felt her blood rushing through her every vein. Her vision seemed both softer and clearer than any time before, able to pick out minuscule flaws in the weave of the pillowcase bulging up next to her but making them part of its charm. Every breath brought strength, though, bringing a warmth that flowed through her and eased every tension she'd ever felt in her life.

4

Robert had to have this woman. Bury himself inside her.

Until this moment, he hadn't felt sure she'd want that much of him. But Mallory's ass clenched in Robert's hands so fiercely it made his heart pound harder than when he'd finished his first marathon. The way her legs jolted against his skull thrilled him, and best of all, he could feel her secret shudders rising straight out of her, through her clit and into his tongue and down into his soul.

She couldn't possibly take that much joy from him, and not want him inside her.

If his cock got any more painfully hard, it'd hold him up off the mattress.

Only when her shaking stopped and she collapsed into a liquid heap did he raise his head enough to put a kiss just barely over the crease onto each thigh. He needed a moment to catch his breath before saying, "Well, I had a great time."

Mallory's laugh was the softest sound he'd ever heard from her. "You did?"

"Oh, yeah."

Her thigh twitched enticingly, the muscles playing against each other.

Robert stayed right where he was, close enough to rest a cheek on her clit if he wanted, but rolled onto one elbow so he could use the other hand to trace the irresistible texture of her inner thigh. How could he be getting more excited, just touching her like this? "I haven't had that much fun since…"

She laughed again. "Since?"

He traced tendons back towards her pussy. Her heady flavor still filled his mouth. "Since never. Yeah, since never."

A smile bloomed on Mallory's face. "That's weird. It's the best I've had since never, too."

How could he he feel so absurdly exposed? He still had his pants and socks on. His head was inches from Mallory's pussy, and could still taste her heady flavor all through his mouth.

With her so intimately open to him, how could he be feeling so naked before her?

The words pressing at his heart threatened to make him feel more naked still. He didn't dare think about them too much. "Truth is, I enjoyed that. I really enjoy making you come. I want to do it again and again."

Mallory's gaze didn't leave him. "You mean hodling?"

"No!" Some people only had transactions with one person, but that really cut their profitability. Unique nervous signals were the whole key to blockchain computations and proof of ecstasy. Hodling wasn't only bad finance, it was kind of perverse. "I mean, I'd like to see you again sometime, sure, but I mean here. Now."

Mallory's smile lifted his heart. "We can arrange that. But I have to handle something first."

"Oh?"

"Yep." Mallory lifted her legs and rolled to the side. Robert couldn't help feeling a flash of loss at her retreat before she said, "This has all been one sided." She rolled to her hands and knees, sinking into the bed as she crawled to him.

"Hey," Robert said. "I wasn't done!"

Mallory's fierce kiss burned all the way to his toes. It wasn't as desperate as before, but it felt irresistible. Her tongue surged between his teeth, not forcefully but insistently, slowly rasping against his. The most determined kiss he'd ever felt. A soft groan escaped from him.

She pulled back. "Was that a whimper?"

Robert's head swam. "Uh, no?"

"Uh huh." Mallory's hand on his shoulder felt just as soft as her mouth, but pushed with a strength far beyond what her muscles could support.

41

Robert let her ease him onto his back. He couldn't peel his gaze from her sleek form as she crawled past, her motion hampered by the plushness of the mattress.

Mallory stopped when her face hovered right over the bulge in the front of his suit pants. "This is a transaction, right?"

His cock was jammed up so hard it hurt. Robert almost feared if the pressure got any worse, it might snap. "Yeah."

Mallory looked over her shoulder at him. "And I really want to transact." She opened her mouth wide and ran her upper lip across the bulge in his pants.

It felt nice.

Not great. Nice.

But the way she kept her promise-filled eyes on his the whole time made Robert tremble.

Mallory lifted her mouth and rested her hand lightly on his stomach, right above his belt. Her thumb eased beneath his waistband, tracing a line of fire that sucked his soul into that one spot. "Are you going to make me suck you right through these pants? Or are you going to cooperate?"

Robert fumbled for his belt.

His hands shook too much to work the clasp.

He'd spent every moment in this hotel room suppressing his driving need to strip off his clothes and plunge balls-deep into Mallory. Ravishing her with his hands and tongue had thrilled him, yes, but he'd had to keep a tight rein on himself the whole time. The struggle had paid off, was paying off, right now, and the thought was enough to scramble his nerves.

And that damned belt buckle just wouldn't surrender.

"Give me that," Mallory said, pushing his hands aside.

She deftly unlatched the buckle—maybe that's why women's clothes fastened the opposite way from men's, so that when you really needed it, you could unwrap each other without too much fumbling. Opening the belt exposed the buttons of his fly. Her hand traced his hard bulge again.

Before tonight, he'd had no idea he could moan like that.

Her fingers caressed the top button, tantalizingly close to his cock.

Stray thoughts sparked in his mind. "Should say," he gasped.

Mallory tugged the button free. "If it's anything other than how much you want me to swallow you whole, I don't care."

"Your outfit." Her fingers were brushing right over his cock, and pure madness boiled his blood. "Better than mine."

"Oh?" She gave that tight smile of wicked delight again, and almost assaulted the buttons.

The relief he felt as his strained cock finally escaped the confining trousers and rose free made him sigh with relief. He still couldn't take his gaze off Mallory's face, though.

"Well." Mallory's voice sounded impossibly cheerful as she studied his red, aching cock. "That's convenient." Robert had always felt embarrassed of how his cock rose at the least convenient time, but right now, when it stood more erect than it ever had before, he saw nothing but anticipation in her expression.

She studied him for a moment, like an artist contemplating her materials, then leaned forward, opened her mouth, and without a pause slid her lips right over the head.

The sensation of her tongue circling his tip lit his whole body aflame.

Robert's back arched like he was having a seizure, and he felt his hands twisting into claws to dig at his own flanks. His muscles weren't obeying his mind any more. They only obeyed his cock, and his cock answered to nothing but Mallory's hard suck at his shaft. He coughed in a breath, then wheezed it out. His every instinct shrieked to grab her head, to stroke her head, to move his hips and push himself deeper into her, but he'd never known a woman to like that so he clamped his hands beneath his arching back so they'd have something to pull against and let out a gasp just short of a howl.

Mallory wrapped her fingers around the base of his shaft and retreated so her lips just barely touched his tip as she spoke. "You sure you like that?"

He tried to speak, but his throat seemed to be choked with rocks.

Her teasing tongue flicked out, flicking wet heat across the head. "Maybe you don't?"

It took all Robert's willpower to unclamp his grip. Draw one quivering hand forth. And gently caress her hair, right above her ear.

Mallory offered that wicked little smile again, spread her lips, and keeping one eye locked on Robert's face, slowly slid her lips back down over him.

Robert's heart pounded so forcefully he thought it

might burst through his ribs.

Sucking him deep, Mallory gave her own little groan.

The sound seemed to surround Robert, engulf him just as her lips had, race through him, and dissolve any hope of thought.

5

Mallory could feel the exact moment Robert surrendered. One second his face showed rampant tension, an impossible struggle for self-control. The next, his eyes rolled back and his face went slack. His dick felt like impossibly stiff beneath her lips, hardness covered in soft, slippery skin, his early stickiness salty and a little bitter but not harsh.

When she tightened her lips around his shaft and sucked, hard, he spasmed.

She traced his balls with a finger. He groaned.

She caressed the tip of his cock with her tongue, and his whole body knotted with delight.

Mallory had never really enjoyed giving head, but the chance to return the explosive pleasure he'd given her filled her with delight. She felt dizzy with lust, anchored to reality only by Robert's shaft transfixing her lips.

Beneath her fingers, his balls twitched.

The man was close. If she kept going, he'd explode in moments.

The question was, where did she want that to happen?

Modern refractory treatment gave him three, maybe four climaxes during the transaction. Mallory had to spend them carefully.

She wouldn't mind him coming in her mouth. She'd take a certain glee in running her tongue all over the head of his cock as he spasmed, inflicting tortuous joy for every second of his orgasm. And a few seconds after, too. Just to give him more than a man could stand. To show him who really owned his dick.

She enjoyed the thought enough to make her tingle.

She was going to enjoy inflicting that delight on him even more.

But as she thought it, she pulled her mouth off of him.

Robert gave a cry just short of a shout and sagged into the mattress.

She had an impulse to run her finger up to the the head of his dick before letting go, but no. She didn't want to tip him over the edge.

Not yet.

Her body had its own tremors, its own desperate needs. He'd just spent who knows how long with her clit, and it begged for more.

Careful to not touch his loaded, swollen cock she slid up, tickling her own breasts against his abs and pecs.

He was drawing long breaths, trying to reassert his control. Mallory waited for him to haul in a lungful of air, then pressed her mouth to his and caressed his gums with her tongue. His strong arms eased around her, dragging her against him. One hand glided down to her ass to pull her closer.

Mallory wrapped herself close, enjoying how the heat of his abs rose into her and the way his hard cock pushed against her thigh. His ankle curled over hers, trapping her, and she gave herself to the kiss.

He broke it off sooner than she wanted. His eyes stared into hers with desperately restrained lust.

Mallory kissed the edge of his mouth, then worked her way back towards Robert's bright red ear. "Tease me."

Robert's hand trailed up her spine.

"No." She leaned closer, breathing the words against his earlobe. "Your cock. Tease my clit with your cock."

Like lightning, Robert rolled her to her flank. One hand pulled her leg over his side, then he slid up to align their bodies. His face flashed past too quickly to kiss.

His sudden movement stunned her. Even if she'd changed her mind, she wouldn't have had a chance to breathe a word.

He reached between them to aim his cock right where she wanted it.

She lit up.

His tongue had felt spectacular.

His cock felt better.

He worked it as he had his tongue, gentle clockwise circles that explored up and down her crack. Where his tongue had been all wet softness, though, his cock brought its own slipperiness with its velvety strength.

When he brought himself to her clit, her moan dragged an echoing groan from Robert.

The urge, the desperate mewling *need*, to shift her hips forward and pull him inside rampaged through her. Her inner walls felt the lightning in her clit and screamed for their own attention.

She felt so ready for him.

But she wasn't ready for him to take himself off her electric clit.

Mallory raised her mouth to kiss him again, but his lips were just a little bit too far up, so she attacked his neck and chest instead, kissing and gnawing and digging her fingers into his muscular back. Robert's arm trapped between them added just a touch of annoyance to her passion. She ached to pull him to her, to feel his full body pressed tight against her, all the way into her, but that interfering arm was the price for the slow, delicious circles massaging her clit and sending spirals of pleasure out through her. A sudden spike of sensation hammered up from her pussy to her spine. She reflexively clamped her teeth down on Robert's chest, eliciting a howl from him.

His free arm drew her closer, crushing air from her, but she only had attention for the explosion building in her center.

The orgasm seized her.

The world turned white. Nothing but delicious quivering surges of passion rupturing from her center and the taste of Robert's sweat and his smell, touches of cinnamon as he bent to crash his lips into hers, capturing her cries in his mouth like he needed to suck her into himself as she burned to wholly engulf him, one crash after another.

She needed him. Nothing mattered but his cock slipping into her.

Inches from her eyes, Robert's face mirrored her

own lust.

Reflected her own delightful, insane, all-consuming need.

Unable to even think, Mallory found the strength to rock her hips forward and up, slipping his cock off her clit and barely into her. Only enough that she could feel the pressure as his cock opened her. Enough to make every inch inside her demand its own chances to feel him.

Robert's back arched. His head rolled back as he cried out wordlessly.

Mallory tugged his arm trapped between them, feebly trying to pull it out of their way.

Robert yanked his arm out in a flash, seizing her to roll on top.

Rabid lust twisted his face into a snarl and a scowl and a smile all at once, eyes intent on her as his arms engulfed her. His hips shifted, driving him a sweet inch deeper into her.

They both cried out together.

Her hips rocked. She wasn't working them, wasn't thinking of that motion, but they knew what to do.

A shred of her remembered that he'd been trying to make things nice for her.

That fragmentary thought only fed her need.

She wrapped her legs around his ass, raising her hips to his and dragging him into her pussy in a single firm, inexorable thrust.

Nature took over.

She rolled onto him, thrusting her tongue into his mouth as deeply as he penetrated her, rocking her hips to guide exactly where his cock stroked her inner walls.

Her explosions rippled through him, driving more frenzy into his thrusts. He sat up and pulled her to him, sucking her breasts as he bounced her on his thighs, triggering gasping ecstatic sobs, before he rolled her over and mercilessly, deliciously rode her, sweat-slicked together.

Each stroke brought its own overlapping echoes of ecstasy.

6

Robert only became aware of himself when he felt his own pressure building, his balls beginning to twitch and spasm. Mallory writhed with each thrust. The most beautiful moment of his life. Desperately unwilling to stop fucking, he managed to gasp, "Roll over."

She didn't ask, only separated her knees so she could roll without releasing his cock. She barely had her knees planted before she rose straight, pushing herself down hard to bury him deep within her.

Robert trembled. His cock felt impossibly heavy and tender, caressed by Mallory's every secret twitch. He gathered his will to gasp, "Close."

His Mallory, and she was his now, totally his, gave that little smile. She rocked herself forward, slipping herself over his cock, and lowered herself to plant a gentle kiss on his lips. "Good."

Her hips rolled back, driving him deep again.

His fingers spasmed and dug into her hips.

She began rocking, quickly engulfing before sliding up just short of releasing him, moving faster and faster.

"Not done," he coughed.

"Fuck you," Mallory said, half-laughing, half gasping. "Fuck me, fuck. Fuck." Her long fingers clenched his chest, drawing lines of fire into his pecs and making his heart thrum even more. "Need you. Need."

Those words were too much.

Robert detonated, back arching, hips rising to hold himself deep within Mallory. Pulse after shattering pulse rocketed through him, scraping away everything but the sensation of being buried within her. Her low, long cries echoed down her body, mirroring his higher-pitched groan of ecstasy.

His cock nailed to heaven, he couldn't even breathe.

When he sagged, Mallory followed him down.

Keeping him trapped within her.

Robert gasped.

He slipped a little when she leaned forward to sprawl on his chest and give him a slow, gentle kiss, but she still had his tip wonderfully imprisoned.

They lay in communal sweat for moments, focused on simple breathing. Letting the storms them clear naturally. Passion spent, each enjoying the other's animal presence.

Minutes or years later, Robert found he had one hand over her back, holding her close, while the fingers of the other traced up and down the inside of her ass.

He needed another eternity to assemble a word. "So."

Mallory giggled. "So. Yeah."

"Not that I have anything to compare against." Even with Robert's lust burned to ashes, the easy intimacy of touching Mallory felt wonderful. "But I think we at least broke even."

The way Mallory stiffened devastated him. "Do you want to check?" she said.

"No!" Checking their NookieCoin balance meant ending the transaction.

Robert wanted to have Mallory sprawled on top of him forever.

Her tension faded. Mostly.

"Not now," he said. "Eventually." He let his fingers trail up her spine, and back down to her ass. "Very eventually."

"Good." She raised her head. Sweat had dried in her short hair. Her face had a happy flush, and the smile on her face looked more completely open than he'd ever seen from anyone. "So." Her face picked up a little grin. "What shall we do until then?"

Robert let his other hand caress her neck, right along the strand of pearls. The other he let trail even lower, brushing right up against where she held him. He only needed a light pressure to feel himself through her, a whole new intimacy. "Personally, I'm starving."

Mallory shifted her hips as if to try to squeeze him.

The motion finally dislodged his cock.

Robert couldn't help a sigh.

"Can't last forever," Mallory rolled to the side. The sudden cool air across his hot skin shocked him. "Or we'd starve." She wrapped herself against his side. "You wanted food? There's a tray here. Sandwiches."

"Sandwiches sound wonderful." He cradled her in his arm.

"Maybe a shower," Mallory said.

"There's a problem with that."

"The shower's amazing."

"I'm sure it is." Robert squeezed her. "But you promised to let me touch all of you, and I only got the front."

"Maybe you should come into the shower with me, then."

"That might work. Does it look slippery?"

Mallory's hand brushing across his chest sent quiet shivers through him. "Slippery?"

"Yeah. The floor, I mean. Because eventually you'll need to brace yourself."

Her hand moved down and gently squeezed. "I can brace myself on this."

Robert let himself enjoy her touch, and the faint stirrings that said he wasn't finished.

"We can do that." He caressed the side of her tit. "And that chair over there doesn't have any arms. Straddling me on it would be a lot easier than on this bed." His finger traced her areolae. "And I'd get some serious time with these."

"We can do that." Mallory released him. "But sometime in all this, I'm going to need you to come in my mouth." Gleeful malice touched her smile. "I have plans."

"We'll probably need another shower after all that."

"That's fine. You can nail me to the wall."

Robert couldn't help a chuckle. "I'm in shape, but do you want them to carry me out of here tomorrow?"

"Not too early. I got us three PM check-out."

He laughed. "Two-thirty it is."

7

They barely escaped the room before the cleaning bots vacuumed over them.

Rather than get back in the rumpled dress, Mallory had opted for the hotel's disposable shirt, slacks, and sandals. She ached—not just inside, or in her jaw, but her legs and back and arms and neck and everything, everywhere.

Robert had put his suit in a bag and picked out another set of disposables. His straight posture made them look pretty good, but his smile when he looked at her made him look fantastic.

Until he walked. Then his obvious aches gave her a sense of pride.

Walking out of the hotel room shadowed her mood. He didn't look unhappy, but more… pensive? On the way to the elevator, his gaze kept darting to her face and dancing away.

Shy, for someone who'd seen more of her than anyone.

When Robert walked away, Mallory might never see him again. Not that she was looking to hodl him—she wasn't a creep. But everyone said you always remembered your first transaction, and she couldn't imagine forgetting Robert.

But she thought that the longer she put off ending the transaction, the more she delayed, the worse she'd feel.

And the worse she felt, the more meager the transaction.

They might have scored big, shot the moon. She hadn't done anything to prevent that. But even if everything went perfectly, they wouldn't have anything definite for nine and a half months. She wouldn't get a new coin until the child's first birthday.

Leaving the elevator into the swank lobby, before she had to watch Robert walk away, Mallory blinked each eye alternately, twice. "Blockchain computation end."

The lobby desk announced in a smoothly cultured voice. "The One Night Holiday Inn congratulates you on your first transaction, and hopes you will remember us for all your future needs."

Thankfully, Robert stopped.

All traces of his smile had evaporated, and his gem-green eyes looked as serious as at their first meeting. That was modern life, though. You transacted, you profitably enjoyed yourself, you moved on.

Saying goodbye was polite, but once the transaction ended, they didn't need anything else.

It's not like sex had anything to do with love or friendship. Civilization had improved once people realized relationships and sex simply weren't compatible.

Her throat felt heavy. "I had a really nice time."

"I did too." Robert's voice had returned to formality as well.

That was probably best.

She should go back to her apartment. She'd planned to have dinner with Alice tonight. Her sister would want to know the story, and what was she going to say? *It was nice. We said goodbye. It's done.*

Mallory's implant buzzed behind her ear, giving three short gasps she'd never heard before. The blockchain had finished processing their transaction and had returned the result.

From the way Robert's eyes widened, she could tell he'd gotten the same signal.

She froze.

This was her very last opportunity to say anything to Robert before money really entered their lives.

Before she could think, Mallory blurted "Hey. Before we look at that."

Robert cocked his head.

Her heart was beating almost as fast as it had when Robert had first touched her. And was that nervous sweat on her back?

She didn't want to be a hodler or, worse, a stalker. Any kind of asshole, really.

Yes, a really profitable transaction would be reason to see him again.

But she didn't really care how profitable the transaction had been.

And her delay in speaking only amplified the curious look on Robert's face.

Was that a little anguish in his face?

Was he worried she was going to say something to ruin their night?

But she really wanted—no, she *needed* to see him again.

She was going to ruin everything.

She'd spoken, so she had to say something.

She'd committed himself.

Robert burst out with, "I'd kind of like to see you

again sometime. Not, uh, next week, but—you know. Sometime. I mean, no matter what the blockchain says. I had a really great time."

He clamped his mouth shut.

Mallory's heart beat hummingbird-quick against her ribs.

His face plunged.

She could see his fear that he'd screwed up as clearly as if he'd painted it on a sign. He didn't want to be creepy, either.

Mallory's face dissolved into a grin.

Robert's eyes got big.

No wonder sex didn't go with relationships. Teasing your partner was… kind of fun.

"You know what?" Mallory said. "Ping me in a few months. We'll schedule something." She glanced around the fancy lobby. "Maybe not this nice."

Robert's face shattered into a beaming smile. "I won't have that kind of wine, either. How do you feel about Chinese?"

Mallory deliberately raised her eyebrows. "Lots of calories. We'll need to work them off."

"I'll do some research," Robert said. "I'm sure there's really… interesting ways to burn off sesame chicken."

"Do that." Mallory leaned forward, pressing her lips to Robert's. The kiss wasn't nearly as thorough as the one they'd shared in before leaving the hotel room, but it warmed her in a way that had nothing to do with her libido.

Maybe the blockchain improved sex, but it seemed to help fondness as well.

Or maybe, despite everything she'd been taught, did

fondness improve sex?

Robert's hand came up to cradle her cheek. "Take care of yourself."

Mallory leaned into his warmth for a moment. "You too." She grinned. "And that exercise you do? Keep it up. You'll need it."

Robert offered a smile. "Me? I'm going to leave you a wet dishrag."

"You're on."

Robert picked up the bag containing his suit and the empty wine bottle.

Heart infinitely lighter, Mallory watched him retreat across the long lobby towards the door. She didn't take a step until he vanished outside.

The hotel lobby didn't feel only vacant, but utterly empty.

Outside, Mallory stopped under the awning. In the twenty-four hours she'd spent inside the hotel, the whole world felt like it had changed. The sun shone. The sky still looked blue.

But everything had changed.

Robert stood on the sidewalk a couple dozen yards away, staring at his palmtop. Was he waiting for her? No, he wasn't that rude.

He looked… stunned?

A frisson ran down Mallory's spine.

The transaction.

He'd checked their earnings.

Trepidation turned her insides muddy.

She'd had a fantastic night.

They couldn't have blown it.

Could they?

She'd hoped to earn ten percent on this. They'd exchanged a tenth of a NookieCoin. Ten percent on that would be point oh one NkC.

What had they achieved? Five percent?

Two?

What kind of sex did people have, anyway?

Trying to ignore her thunderous pulse, Mallory fumbled her own palmtop out of her bag. She needed two tries to swipe the biometric reader, but eventually the screen unlocked.

Had they gone negative?

She could barely poke the blinking red icon of her NookieCoin client.

Her breath stopped.

She'd hoped for ten percent.

The screen read: TRANSACTION PROCEEDS: 35.8719346211%.

BALANCE 1.0358719346211 NkC.

Mallory made herself swallow.

Thirty-five percent?

Almost four times what she'd hoped for?

She looked up.

Up the sidewalk, Robert was staring at her.

His gaze met hers.

Yes, hanging around after a transaction was crass. He wasn't trying to creep at her, though. His astonishment crossed the chasm between them.

Embarrassment flushed Robert's face.

He turned to walk away.

A lump the size of a lemon swelled in Mallory's throat.

In the hotel lobby, he'd put himself out there. He'd said what he wanted.

And what he wanted was her. Again.

The least she could do was take the same chance for him.

"Robert!" she shouted.

He looked over his shoulder, surprised.

Mallory trotted up to him, bag swinging from her hand.

"Hey," Robert said uncertainly.

"Next time?" Mallory said. "That three months?"

"Yeah?"

She took a deep breath. "Can we make it a month?"

If her sister thought less of her, that transaction would shut her up.

The unease dissolved from Robert's face. "A month it is."

She grinned. "And I'm wearing something you can rip off me."

"That sounds wonderful." She glimpsed his smile before he turned to walk away. "This time, I'm gonna make *you* keep it on for a while."

About the Author

https://www.michaelwarrenlucas.com

Never miss another new release!

Sign up for Michael Warren Lucas' mailing list at

http://mwl.io.

Twitter: @mwlauthor

Mastodon: mwlucas@bsd.network

www.ingramcontent.com/pod-product-compliance
Lightning Source LLC
Chambersburg PA
CBHW071212130626
46555CB00004B/1681